First published in the United States 1991 by Chronicle Books.
Copyright © 1985 by Taro Gomi.
All rights reserved. No part of this book may be reproduced in any form without written permission from the publisher.
Jacket and book design by Giorgio Baravalle
Printed in Singapore.

Originally published in Japanese by Kaisei-sha, Tokyo under the title, "KOTOBA ZUKAN 1—Ugoki no Kotoba." English translation rights arranged with Kaisei-sha Publishing through Japan Foreign Rights Centre.

Gomi, Taro.
    [Ugoki no kotoba. English]
    Seeing, saying, doing, playing : a big book of action words / by Taro Gomi.
        p.   cm.
    Summary: Labeled illustrations show people performing everyday activities, including eating, sleeping, dressing, and playing.
    ISBN 0-87701-859-6
    1. English language—Gerund—Juvenile literature.   2. Vocabulary—Juvenile literature.
[1. English language—Verb.   2. Vocabulary.]   I. Title.
PE1313.G6513   1985   90-47402
428.1—dc20   CIP
                                                                                      AC

Distributed in Canada by Raincoast books, 112 East 3rd Avenue, Vancouver B.C., V5T 1C8

10 9 8 7 6 5 4 3 2 1

Chronicle Books
275 Fifth Street
San Francisco, California 94103

SINGING

PLAYING

WISHING

STRETCHING

SERVING

PURRING

PRAYING

CLAPPING

OPENING

WAITING

CELEBRATING

DROWSING

PRESENTING

POURING

THANKING

TELLING

LISTENING

SURPRISING

DANGLING

HIDING

SCRATCHING

RUNNING

SEEING, SAYING, DOING, PLAYING

A big book of action words
by Taro Gomi

Chronicle Books • San Francisco

RUNNING   LOOKING   READING   SNOOPING   WAITING

WALKING

SCURRYING

TYING

SWEEPING

WAXING

FILLING

HURRYING   GOSSIPING

DRESSING

DRAGGING

GRIMACING

YAWNING

WALKING

WATCHING   REPORTING

BRUSHING

RINSING

CALLING

3

REMOVING

HANGING

DECORATING

RETURNING

UNROLLING

PULLING

HOLDING

STRAIGHTENING

KICKING

DRUMMING

SINGING

PLAYING

CHASING

FIGHTING

TICKLING

WINCING

HITTING

FLEEING

SPELLING

MOLDING

STRINGING

WHOOPING

SNIFFING

SCOLDING

PRODDING

CRAWLING

SLEEPING

STACKING

SCATTERING

PLAYING

CLOSING

FLYING

JUMPING

LEAPING

RIDING

WATCHING

MOUNTING

HOPPING

CHASING

FLUTTERING

CHASING

TRIPPING

RUBBING

CLINGING

CLIMBING

HANGING

FROWNING

POKING

KNOTTIN

HISSING

SHRIEKING

SLITHERING

FRIGHTENING

ROLLING

SCRATCHING

SPREADING

SPLITTING

OPENING

COOKING

SKEWERING

PEELING

FANNING

DUMPING

DRYING

YELLIN

BOILING

FRYING

SPILLING

CHEWING

YELLING

STUMBLING

BARBECUING

12

EATING

LEADING

LEANING

CHEWING

POINTING

LOOKING

POSING

PAINTING

WAILING

GRAZING

NUZZLING

NIBBLING

ARGUING

WALKING

HUGGING

CHASING

PETTING

EXPLAINING

BRUSHI

TYING

WATCHING

PHOTOGRAPHING

GRUMBLING

LOOKING

IMITATING

PEELING

RUNNING

DEVOURING

SNACKING

ROARING

14

WALKING

STRUTTING

ARRIVING

TIMING

COACHING

RACING

FREEING

ROOTING

FISHING

WATCHING

SITTING

BOATING

ROWING

NETTING

BRICKLAYING

POKING

RUNNING

SPLASHING

SAILING

CLIMBING

WINDING

STROLLING

FEEDING

HIDING

RUNNING

BATTING

SWINGING

SIGNALING

READING

KNITTING

16

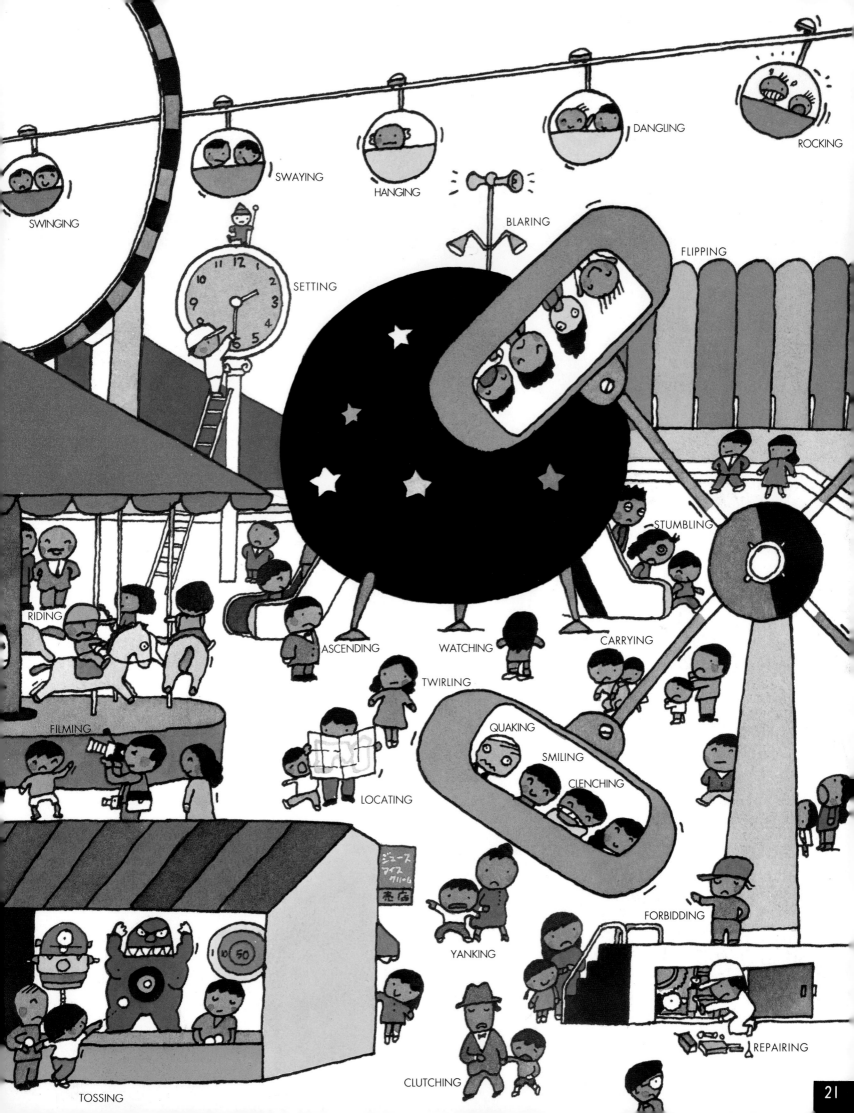

SWINGING

SWAYING

HANGING

BLARING

DANGLING

ROCKING

SETTING

FLIPPING

ASCENDING

WATCHING

STUMBLING

CARRYING

RIDING

TWIRLING

FILMING

QUAKING

SMILING

CLENCHING

LOCATING

FORBIDDING

YANKING

ジュース
アイス
クリーム

売店

REPAIRING

CLUTCHING

TOSSING

21

If you look carefully, you can find all these actions in this book.

Can you find any others?

ACCUSING
ADJUSTING
ADMIRING
ALERTING
ARGUING
ARRIVING
ASCENDING
ASKING
ASSISTING
BALANCING
BATTING
BATTLING
BAWLING
BELLOWING
BENDING
BIKING
BITING
BLOWING
BLOWING BUBBLES
BLUSHING
BOARDING
BOATING
BOILING
BOUNDING
BOWING
BRAKING
BREAKING
BRICKLAYING
BRINGING
BRUSHING
BUCKLING
BUILDING
BUMPING
BUYING
CALLING
CARRYING
CARTWHEELING
CATCHING
CELEBRATING
CHARGING
CHASING
CHATTING
CHECKING
CHEERING
CHEWING
CHIRPING

CHOKING
CHOOSING
CLAPPING
CLEANING
CLENCHING
CLIMBING
CLINGING
CLOSING
CLOWNING
CLUCKING
CLUTCHING
COACHING
COLLECTING
COLLIDING
COMBING
COMFORTING
COMPARING
COOKING
COPYING
CRASHING
CRAWLING
CREEPING
CROSSING
CROWDING
CRYING
CUDDLING
CUTTING
DANCING
DANGLING
DASHING
DAWDLING
DAYDREAMING
DECIDING
DECORATING
DELIVERING
DEVOURING
DIGGING
DIPPING
DIRECTING
DIVING
DRAGGING
DRAWING
DRESSING
DRIFTING
DRINKING
DRIPPING

DROPPING OFF
DROWNING
DROWSING
DRYING
DUMPING
DYEING
EATING
ENJOYING
ENTERING
EXAMINING
EXERCISING
EXITING
EXPLAINING
EXTINGUISHING
EYEING
FALLING
FANNING
FEEDING
FIGHTING
FILLING
FILMING
FISHING
FLEEING
FLIPPING
FLOATING
FLUTTERING
FLYING
FOLDING
FOLLOWING
FORBIDDING
FREEING
FRIGHTENING
FROWNING
FRYING
GAPING
GARDENING
GASPING

GATHERING
GAWKING
GAZING
GETTING OUT
GIVING
GLANCING
GLARING
GLIDING
GOING
GOSSIPING
GRABBING
GRAZING
GREETING
GRILLING
GRIMACING
GRIPPING
GRITTING
GROWLING
GRUMBLING
GUARDING
HAILING
HALTING
HAMMERING
HANGING
HAULING
HELPING
HERDING
HIDING
HIKING
HISSING
HITTING
HOBBLING
HOEING
HOLDING
HOLDING HANDS
HOLLERING
HONKING
HOPPING
HUGGING
HURRYING

IGNORING
IMITATING
INSISTING
INSPECTING
INSTRUCTING
JOGGING
JOINING
JUGGLING
JUMPING
JUMPING ROPE
KICKING
KISSING
KNEELING
KNITTING
KNOCKING
KNOTTING
LACING
LANDING
LAUGHING
LAUNCHING
LEADING
LEANING
LEAPING
LEARNING
LEASHING
LEAVING
LICKING
LIFTING
LIMPING
LISTENING
LOADING
LOCATING
LOCKING
LOOKING
MAILING
MEASURING
MEETING
MIXING
MOLDING
MOOING
MOPING
MOPPING
MUNCHING
NAPPING
NESTING
NETTING
NIBBLING
NOTICING
NUZZLING
OBSERVING
OFFERING
OINKING
OPENING
ORDERING
PACKING

PAINTING
PARADING
PATTING
PAYING
PEEKING
PEELING
PEERING
PERSUADING
PETTING
PHOTOGRAPHING
PICKING
PICKING UP
PILING
PIROUETTING
PITCHING
PLACING
PLANTING
PLAYING
PLUNGING
POINTING
POKING
POSING
POUNDING
POURING
PRACTICING
PRAYING
PRESENTING
PRETENDING
PRODDING
PULLING
PUNCHING
PUNISHING
PURRING
PUSHING
QUAKING
RACING
RAINING
REACHING
READING
RECEIVING
RECITING
RECONSIDERING
REFUSING
REGRETTING
RELAXING
REMOVING
RENTING
REPACKING
REPAIRING

REPORTING
REPRIMANDING
RESCUING
RESISTING
RESTING
RETURNING
RIDING
RINSING
RIPPING
ROAMING
ROASTING
ROCKING
ROLLER SKATING
ROLLING
ROOTING
ROWING
RUBBING
RUNNING
RUSHING
SAILING
SAUNTERING
SAWING
SCAMPERING
SCARING
SCATTERING
SCOLDING
SCOOPING
SCOOTING
SCRATCHING
SCREAMING
SCREECHING
SCURRYING
SEARCHING
SELLING
SERVING
SETTING
SEWING
SHAKING
SHAKING HANDS
SHARING
SHAVING
SHINING
SHIVERING
SHOOTING
SHOULDERING
SHOUTING
SHOVING
SHOWERING
SHOWING
SHRIEKING
SHUSHING
SIGHTSEEING
SIGNALING
SINGING

SINKING
SIPPING
SITTING
SKATING
SKEWERING
SKIPPING
SLAPPING
SLEEP WALKING
SLEEPING
SLICING
SLIDING
SLIPPING
SLITHERING
SMELLING
SMILING
SMOKING
SNACKING
SNAPPING
SNATCHING
SNEAKING
SNIFFLING
SNOOPING
SNOOZING
SOMERSAULTING
SOBBING
SORTING
SOWING
SPEAKING
SPEEDING
SPELLING
SPILLING
SPLASHING
SPLITTING
SPOONING
SPREADING
SPRINGING
SPRINTING
SQUEALING
SQUEEZING
SQUINTING
STACKING
STALKING
STANDING
STARING

STEADYING
STEALING
STEPPING
STIRRING
STOPPING
STRAIGHTENING
STRETCHING
STRINGING
STROLLING
STRUTTING
STUMBLING
SUCKLING
SUGGESTING
SULKING
SUNNING
SURPRISING
SWAYING
SWEEPING
SWERVING
SWIMMING
SWIMMING UNDERWATER
SWINGING
TALKING
TAPING
TAPPING
TASTING
TEACHING
TEARING
TEASING
TELEPHONING
TELLING
TESTING
THANKING
THROWING
TICKLING
TILTING
TIMING
TIPPING
TODDLING
TOSSING
TOUCHING
TOWELING
TRADING
TRAILING

TRIPPING
TRYING
TUGGING
TURNING
TWIRLING
TYING
UNCOVERING
UNDRESSING
UNROLLING
VEERING
VIEWING
VISITING
WADING
WAILING
WAITING
WAKING
WALKING
WARMING
WARNING
WASHING
WATCHING
WAVING
WAXING
WEARING
WEEDING
WEIGHING
WELCOMING
WHISPERING
WHISTLING
WHOOPING
WIGGLING
WINCING
WINDING
WIPING
WISHING
WOBBLING
WONDERING
WORKING
WORRYING
WRAPPING
WRINGING
YANKING
YAWNING
YELLING
YELPING
ZIPPING
ZOOMING